The
VELVETEEN
RABBIT
& Other Stories

The
VELVETEEN
RABBIT
& Other Stories

HarperFestival®
A Division of HarperCollins*Publishers*

HarperCollins®, ☎®, and HarperFestival®
are trademarks of HarperCollins Publishers.

The Velveteen Rabbit & Other Stories
www.harpercollinschildrens.com

Library of Congress catalog card number: 2007930293
ISBN 978-0-06-145942-9
Typography by Sasha Illingworth
1 2 3 4 5 6 7 8 9 10

❖

First HarperFestival edition, 2008.

Contents

The
VELVETEEN
RABBIT
& Other Stories

The Velveteen Rabbit

There was once a velveteen rabbit, and in the beginning he was really splendid. He was fat and bunchy, as a rabbit should be; his coat was spotted brown and white, he had real thread whiskers, and his ears were lined with pink sateen. On Christmas morning, when he sat wedged in the top of the Boy's stocking, with a sprig of holly between his paws, the effect was charming.

There were other things in the stocking,

nuts and oranges and a toy engine, and chocolate almonds and a clockwork mouse, but the Rabbit was quite the best of all. For at least two hours the Boy loved him, and then Aunts and Uncles came to dinner, and there was a great rustling of tissue paper and unwrapping of parcels, and in the excitement of looking at all the new presents the Velveteen Rabbit was forgotten.

For a long time he lived in the toy cupboard or on the nursery floor, and no one thought very much about him. He was naturally shy, and being only made of velveteen, some of the more expensive toys quite snubbed him. The mechanical toys were very superior, and looked down upon every one else; they were full of modern ideas, and pretended they were real. The model boat, who had lived through two seasons and lost most of his paint, caught the tone from them and never missed an opportunity of referring to his rigging in technical terms. The Rabbit could not claim to be a model of anything, for he didn't know that real rabbits existed; he thought they were all stuffed with sawdust like himself, and he understood that sawdust was quite out-of-date and should never be mentioned in modern circles. Even Timothy, the jointed wooden lion, who was made by the disabled soldiers, and should have had broader views, put on airs and pretended he was connected with Government. Between them all the poor little Rabbit was made to feel himself very insignificant and commonplace, and the only person who was kind to him at all was the Skin Horse.

The Skin Horse had lived longer in the nursery than any of the others. He was so old that his brown coat was bald in patches and showed the seams underneath, and most of the hairs in his tail had been pulled out to string bead necklaces. He was wise, for he had seen a long succession of mechanical toys arrive to boast and swagger, and by-and-by break their mainsprings and pass away, and he knew that they were only toys, and would never turn into anything else. For nursery magic is very strange and wonderful, and only those playthings that are old and wise and experienced like the Skin

Horse understand all about it.

"What is REAL?" asked the Rabbit one day, when they were lying side by side near the nursery fender, before Nana came to tidy the room. "Does it mean having things that buzz inside you and a stick-out handle?"

"Real isn't how you are made," said the Skin Horse. "It's a thing that happens to you. When a child loves you for a long, long time, not just to play with, but REALLY loves you, then you become Real."

"Does it hurt?" asked the Rabbit.

"Sometimes," said the Skin Horse, for he was always truthful. "When you are Real you don't mind being hurt."

"Does it happen all at once, like being wound up," he asked, "or bit by bit?"

"It doesn't happen all at once," said the Skin Horse. "You become. It takes a long time. That's why it doesn't often happen to people who break easily, or have sharp edges, or who have to be carefully kept. Generally, by the time you are Real, most of your hair has been loved off, and your eyes drop out and you get loose in the joints and very shabby. But these things don't matter at all, because once you are Real you can't be ugly, except to people who don't understand."

"I suppose *you* are Real?" said the Rabbit. And then he wished he had not said it, for he thought the Skin Horse might be sensitive. But the Skin Horse only smiled.

"The Boy's Uncle made me Real," he said. "That was a great many years ago; but

once you are Real you can't become unreal again. It lasts for always."

The Rabbit sighed. He thought it would be a long time before this magic called Real happened to him. He longed to become Real, to know what it felt like; and yet the idea of growing shabby and losing his eyes and whiskers was rather sad. He wished that he could become it without these uncomfortable things happening to him.

There was a person called Nana who ruled the nursery. Sometimes she took no notice of the playthings lying about, and sometimes, for no reason whatever, she went swooping about like a great wind and hustled them away in cupboards. She called this "tidying up," and the playthings all hated it, especially the tin ones. The Rabbit didn't mind it so much, for wherever he was thrown he came down soft.

One evening, when the Boy was going to bed, he couldn't find the china dog that always slept with him. Nana was in a hurry, and it was too much trouble to hunt for china dogs at bedtime, so she simply looked about her, and seeing that the toy cupboard door stood open, she made a swoop.

"Here," she said, "take your old Bunny! He'll do to sleep with you!" And she dragged the Rabbit out by one ear, and put him into the Boy's arms.

That night, and for many nights after, the Velveteen Rabbit slept in the Boy's bed. At first he found it rather uncomfortable, for the Boy hugged him very tight, and sometimes he rolled over on him, and sometimes he pushed him so far under the pillow that the Rabbit could scarcely breathe. And he missed, too, those long moonlight hours in the nursery, when all the house was silent, and his talks with the Skin Horse. But very soon he grew to like it, for the Boy used to talk to him, and made nice tunnels for him under the bedclothes that he said were like the burrows the real rabbits lived in. And they had splendid games together, in whispers, when Nana had gone away to her supper and left the night-light burning on the mantelpiece. And when the Boy dropped off to sleep, the Rabbit would snuggle down close under his little warm chin and dream, with the Boy's hands clasped close round him all night long.

And so time went on, and the little Rabbit was very happy—so happy that he never noticed how his beautiful velveteen fur was getting shabbier and shabbier, and his tail coming unsewn, and all the pink rubbed off his nose where the Boy had kissed him.

Spring came, and they had long days in the garden, for wherever the Boy went the Rabbit went too. He had rides in the wheel-barrow, and picnics on the grass, and lovely fairy huts built for him under the raspberry canes behind the flower border. And once, when the Boy was called away suddenly to go out to tea, the Rabbit was left out on the lawn until long after dusk, and Nana had to come and look for him with the candle because the Boy couldn't go to sleep unless he was there. He was wet through with the dew and quite earthy from diving into the burrows the Boy had made for him in the flower bed, and Nana grumbled as she rubbed him off with a corner of her apron.

"You must have your old Bunny!" she said. "Fancy all that fuss for a toy!"

The Boy sat up in bed and stretched out his hands.

"Give me my Bunny!" he said. "You mustn't say that. He isn't a toy. He's REAL!"

When the little Rabbit heard that, he was happy, for he knew that what the Skin Horse had said was true at last. The nursery magic had happened to him, and he was a toy no

longer. He was Real. The Boy himself had said it.

That night he was almost too happy to sleep, and so much love stirred in his little sawdust heart that it almost burst. And into his boot-button eyes, that had long ago lost their polish, there came a look of wisdom and beauty, so that even Nana noticed it next morning when she picked him up, and said, "I declare if that old Bunny hasn't got quite a knowing expression!"

That was a wonderful Summer!

Near the house where they lived there was a wood, and in the long June evenings the Boy liked to go there after tea to play. He took the Velveteen Rabbit with him, and before he wandered off to pick flowers, or play at brigands among the trees, he always made the Rabbit a little nest somewhere among the bracken, where he would be quite cosy, for he was a kind-hearted little boy and he liked Bunny to be comfortable. One evening, while the Rabbit was lying there alone, watching the ants that ran to and fro between his velvet paws in the grass, he saw two strange beings creep out of the tall bracken near him.

They were rabbits like himself, but quite furry and brand-new. They must have been very well made, for their seams didn't show at all, and they changed shape in a queer way when they moved; one minute they were long and thin and the next minute fat and bunchy, instead of always staying the

same like he did. Their feet padded softly on the ground, and they crept quite close to him, twitching their noses, while the Rabbit stared hard to see which side the clockwork stuck out, for he knew that people who jump generally have something to wind them up. But he couldn't see it. They were evidently a new kind of rabbit altogether.

They stared at him, and the little Rabbit stared back. And all the time their noses twitched.

"Why don't you get up and play with us?" one of them asked.

"I don't feel like it," said the Rabbit, for he didn't want to explain that he had no clockwork.

"Ho!" said the furry rabbit. "It's as easy

as anything." And he gave a big hop sideways and stood on his hind legs.

"I don't believe you can!" he said.

"I can!" said the little Rabbit. "I can jump
higher than anything!" He meant when the
Boy threw him, but of course he didn't want
to say so.

"Can you hop on your hind legs?" asked
the furry rabbit.

That was a dreadful question, for the
Velveteen Rabbit had no hind legs at all!
The back of him was made all in one piece,
like a pincushion. He sat still in the bracken,
and hoped that the other rabbits wouldn't
notice.

"I don't want to!" he said again.

But the wild rabbits have very sharp

eyes. And this one stretched out his neck and looked.

"He hasn't got any hind legs!" he called out. "Fancy a rabbit without any hind legs!" And he began to laugh.

"I have!" cried the little Rabbit. "I have got hind legs! I am sitting on them!"

"Then stretch them out and show me, like this!" said the wild rabbit. And he began to whirl round and dance, till the little Rabbit got quite dizzy.

"I don't like dancing," he said. "I'd rather sit still!"

But all the while he was longing to dance, for a funny new tickly feeling ran through him, and he felt he would give anything in the world to be able to jump about like these rabbits did.

The strange rabbit stopped dancing, and came quite close. He came so close this time that his long whiskers brushed the Velveteen Rabbit's ear, and then he wrinkled his nose suddenly and flattened his ears and jumped backwards.

"He doesn't smell right!" he exclaimed. "He isn't a rabbit at all! He isn't real!"

"I *am* Real!" said the little Rabbit. "I am Real! The Boy said so!" And he nearly began to cry.

Just then there was a sound of footsteps, and the Boy ran past near them, and with a stamp of feet and a flash of white tails the two strange rabbits disappeared.

"Come back and play with me!" called the

little Rabbit. "Oh, do come back! I *know* I am Real!"

But there was no answer, only the little ants ran to and fro, and the bracken swayed gently where the two strangers had passed. The Velveteen Rabbit was all alone.

"Oh, dear!" he thought. "Why did they run away like that? Why couldn't they stop and talk to me?"

For a long time he lay very still, watching the bracken, and hoping that they would come back. But they never returned, and presently the sun sank lower and the little white moths fluttered out, and the Boy came and carried him home.

Weeks passed, and the little Rabbit grew very old and shabby, but the Boy loved him just as much. He loved him so hard that he loved all his whiskers off, and the pink lining to his ears turned grey, and his brown spots faded. He even began to lose his shape, and he scarcely looked like a rabbit any more, except to the Boy. To him he was always beautiful, and that was all that the little Rabbit cared about. He didn't mind how he looked to other people, because the nursery magic had made him Real, and when you are Real, shabbiness doesn't matter.

And then, one day, the Boy was ill.

His face grew very flushed, and he talked in his sleep, and his little body was so hot that it burned the Rabbit when he held him close. Strange people came and went in the

nursery, and a light burned all night and through it all the little Velveteen Rabbit lay there, hidden from sight under the bed-clothes, and he never stirred, for he was afraid that if they found him some one might take him away, and he knew that the Boy needed him.

It was a long weary time, for the Boy was too ill to play, and the little Rabbit found it rather dull with nothing to do all day long. But he snuggled down patiently, and looked forward to the time when the Boy should be well again, and they would go out in the garden amongst the flowers and the butter-flies and play splendid games in the rasp-berry thicket like they used to. All sorts of delightful things he planned, and while the

Boy lay half asleep he crept up close to the pillow and whispered them in his ear. And presently the fever turned, and the Boy got better. He was able to sit up in bed and look at picture books, while the little Rabbit cuddled close at his side. And one day, they let him get up and dress.

It was a bright, sunny morning, and the windows stood wide open. They had carried the Boy out on to the balcony, wrapped in a shawl, and the little Rabbit lay tangled up among the bedclothes, thinking.

The Boy was going to the seaside tomorrow. Everything was arranged, and now it only remained to carry out the doctor's orders. They talked about it all, while the little Rabbit lay under the bedclothes, with just his head peeping out, and listened. The room was to be disinfected, and all the books and toys that the Boy had played with in bed must be burnt.

"Hurrah!" thought the little Rabbit. "Tomorrow we shall go to the seaside!" For the Boy had often talked of the seaside, and he wanted very much to see the big waves coming in, and the tiny crabs, and the sand castles.

Just then Nana caught sight of him.

"How about his old Bunny?" she asked.

"*That?*" said the doctor. "Why, it's a mass of scarlet fever germs!—Burn it at once. What? Nonsense! Get him a new one. He mustn't have that any more!"

And so the little Rabbit was put into a

sack with the old picture-books and a lot of rubbish, and carried out to the end of the garden behind the fowl-house. That was a fine place to make a bonfire, only the gardener was too busy just then to attend to it. He had the potatoes to dig and the green peas to gather, but next morning he promised to come quite early and burn the whole lot.

That night the Boy slept in a different bedroom, and he had a new bunny to sleep with him. It was a splendid bunny, all white plush with real glass eyes, but the Boy was too excited to care very much about it. For tomorrow he was going to the seaside, and that in itself was such a wonderful thing that he could think of nothing else.

And while the Boy was asleep, dreaming

of the seaside, the little Rabbit lay among the old picture-books in the corner behind the fowl-house, and he felt very lonely. The sack had been left untied, and so by wriggling a bit he was able to get his head through the opening and look out. He was shivering a little, for he had always been used to sleeping in a proper bed, and by this time his coat had worn so thin and threadbare from hugging that it was no longer any protection to him. Near by he could see the thicket of raspberry canes, growing tall and close like a tropical jungle, in whose shadow he had played with the Boy on bygone mornings. He thought of those long sunlit hours in the garden—how happy they were—and a great sadness came over him. He seemed to see them all pass before him, each more beautiful than the other, the fairy huts in the flower-bed, the quiet evenings in the wood when he lay in the bracken and the little ants ran over his paws; the wonderful day when he first knew that he was Real. He thought of the Skin Horse, so wise and gentle, and all that he had told him. Of what use was it to be loved and lose one's beauty and become Real if it all ended like this? And a tear, a real tear, trickled down his little shabby velvet nose and fell to the ground.

And then a strange thing happened. For where the tear had fallen a flower grew out of the ground, a mysterious flower, not at all like any that grew in the garden. It had slender green leaves the colour of emeralds, and in the center of the leaves a blossom like a golden cup. It was so beautiful that the little Rabbit forgot to cry, and just lay there watching it.

And presently the blossom opened, and out of it there stepped a fairy.

She was quite the loveliest fairy in the whole world. Her dress was of pearl and dew-drops, and there were flowers round her neck and in her hair, and her face was like the most perfect flower, of all. And she came close to the little Rabbit and gathered him up in her arms and kissed him on his velveteen nose that was all damp from crying.

"Little Rabbit," she said, "don't you know who I am?"

The Rabbit looked up at her, and it seemed to him that he had seen her face before, but he couldn't think where.

"I am the nursery magic Fairy," she said. "I take care of all the playthings that the children have loved. When they are old and worn out and the children don't need them any more, then I come and take them away with me and turn them into Real."

"Wasn't I Real before?" asked the little Rabbit.

"You were Real to the Boy," the Fairy said, "because he loved you. Now you shall be Real to every one."

And she held the little Rabbit close in her arms and flew with him into the wood.

It was light now, for the moon had risen.

All the forest was beautiful, and the fronds of the bracken shone like frosted silver. In the open glade between the tree-trunks the wild rabbits danced with their shadows on the velvet grass, but when they saw the Fairy they all stopped dancing and stood round in a ring to stare at her.

"I've brought you a new playfellow," the Fairy said. "You must be very kind to him and teach him all he needs to know in Rabbit-land, for he is going to live with you for ever and ever!"

And she kissed the little Rabbit again and put him down on the grass.

"Run and play, little Rabbit!" she said.

But the little Rabbit sat quite still for a moment and never moved. For when he saw all the wild rabbits dancing around him he suddenly remembered about his hind legs, and he didn't want them to see that he was made all in one piece. He did not know that when the Fairy kissed him that last time she had changed him altogether. And he might have sat there a long time, too shy to move, if just then something hadn't tickled his nose, and before he thought what he was doing he lifted his hind toe to scratch it.

And he found that he actually had hind legs! Instead of dingy velveteen he had brown fur, soft and shiny, his ears twitched by themselves, and his whiskers were so long that they brushed the grass. He gave one leap and the joy of using those hind legs was so great that he went springing about the turf on them, jumping sideways and whirling round as the others did, and he grew so excited that when at last he did stop to look for the Fairy she had gone.

He was a Real Rabbit at last, at home with the other rabbits.

Autumn passed and Winter, and in the Spring, when the days grew warm and sunny, the Boy went out to play in the wood behind the house. And while he was play-ing, two rabbits crept out from the bracken and peeped at him. One of them was brown all over, but the other had strange markings under his fur, as though long ago he had been spotted, and the spots still showed through. And about his little soft nose and his round black eyes there was something familiar, so that the Boy thought to himself:

"Why, he looks just like my old Bunny that was lost when I had scarlet fever!"

But he never knew that it really was his own Bunny, come back to look at the child who had first helped him to be Real.

The Frog Prince

Once upon a time, there lived a king whose daughters were all beautiful, but the youngest was the most beautiful of all. On warm days, the youngest princess liked to sit by the side of a nearby well. When she was bored she would throw a golden ball, her favorite toy, up high and catch it.

One day, the princess's ball rolled straight into the water. She looked inside, but the well was so deep that the bottom could not be seen. She began to cry until a voice said, "What ails you, Princess? You weep so that even a stone would show pity."

The princess looked around and saw a frog stretching forth his big, ugly head from the water.

"I am weeping for my golden ball, which has fallen into the well," she said.

"Do not weep," answered the frog. "I can help you, but what will you give me if I bring your ball up again?"

"Whatever you want, dear frog," said she, "my clothes, my pearls and jewels, and even the golden crown that I am wearing."

The frog answered, "I do not want anything but for you to love me and let me be your friend, and let me sit by you at your little table, and eat off your little golden plate, and drink out of your little cup, and sleep in your little bed. If you will promise me this, I will bring your golden ball up again."

"Oh, yes," said she, "I promise you all you wish, if you will but bring me my ball back again." But she thought, *As if a silly frog could really be a person's friend!*

The frog dove into the water and retrieved the ball. The delighted princess picked it up and ran quickly away.

"Wait!" called the frog. "Take me with you. I can't run as fast as you!" But the princess ran to the castle without looking back.

The next day, while she was dining with the king and all the courtiers, something crept *splish-splash, splish-splash* up the marble staircase, and then knocked at the door and cried, "Princess, open the door for me!" She ran to open the door, and there sat the ugly frog. Frightened, she slammed the door and sat down to dinner again. The king saw plainly that she was afraid and said to her, "Daughter, why are you so afraid? Is there perchance a giant outside who wants to carry you away?"

"It is no giant but a disgusting frog," replied the princess. She explained what had happened at the well. In the meantime, the frog knocked a second time and called for her again.

The king said, "What you promised, you must do. Go and let him in." She went and opened the door, and the frog hopped in and followed her, step by step, to her chair. And so the frog sat by her at the table, ate off her little golden plate, and drank out of her little cup. The frog enjoyed himself, but almost every spoonful the princess ate choked her. After dinner, he said, "Now I am tired. Carry me into your little room, and we will both lie down and go to sleep."

The king's daughter began to cry, for she was afraid of the cold frog and did not want him to sleep in her pretty, clean little bed. But the king grew angry and said, "He helped you when you were in trouble and should not be despised by you now." So she took hold of the frog with two fingers, carried him into her room, and put him on her bed.

The frog said, "Now give me a goodnight

kiss or I will tell your father." The princess shut her eyes and kissed the frog on his clammy cheek. When she opened her eyes, he was no longer a frog but a king's son, with kind and beautiful eyes. The prince told her how he had been bewitched by an evil fairy to live as a frog, and how no one could have delivered him from the well but herself. The next day, the prince and princess celebrated a joyful wedding and went together to rule his kingdom and live happily ever after.

Peter Pan

Late one night, Peter Pan and the fairy Tinker Bell flew across the London sky. They stopped at the window outside the nursery of the Darling house and crept inside. Peter was looking for his shadow. He had left it behind the last time he visited the nursery, when he secretly listened to Wendy Darling tell bedtime stories about his home, Neverland, to her brothers, Michael and John.

Finally, Peter found his shadow. After he

caught it, he tried to sew it back on, but that didn't work. Peter started to cry, which woke up Wendy. She could not believe her eyes. A boy and a fairy were flying around her room!

"Don't be frightened," Peter said. "Will you come to Neverland with me and tell your stories to my friends? I'll teach you to fly!"

Wendy agreed only after he included John and Michael in the fantastic adventure. The fairy Tinker Bell sprinkled her fairy dust over the children, and soon they were all soaring through the sky and over the sea.

"Second to the right, and straight on till morning!" Peter shouted. When they reached Neverland, they found a beautiful island with golden rainbows, blue waterfalls, the Mermaids' Lagoon, and a pirate ship where the evil Captain Hook lived.

Peter Pan took the children to meet his friends, the lost boys. At the Mermaids' Lagoon, Peter saw that Captain Hook had captured the beautiful Princess Tiger Lily. Peter followed Captain Hook to Marooners' Rock, where they had a duel. Peter made Captain Hook fall into the sea, where he was chased away by a crocodile. Tiger Lily was saved!

That wasn't the end of Captain Hook. He kidnapped Tinker Bell and tricked her into telling him the location of Peter's home. He led his band of pirates to capture the lost boys and the Darling children.

Tinker Bell was imprisoned in the pirate ship, but escaped just in time to alert Peter.

She knew that Hook had put poison in Peter's cup, but Peter would not believe her. As he was about to drink it, Tinker Bell quickly flew and drank it all herself. Suddenly, she dropped to the ground, with her light fading rapidly.

"Oh, Tink, did you drink it to save me?" Peter cried. "How can I help you?"

Tinker Bell said weakly, "I can get well again if children believed in fairies."

Peter wasted no time. He thought of the many children who were dreaming of Neverland at that moment, and asked of them all, "Do you believe?" Tinker Bell heard the children murmur "Yes!" in their sleep and felt much better. She was saved!

Peter and the fairy flew to Captain

Hook's pirate ship, where the Darlings and the lost boys were walking the plank. Wendy had just stepped off and was falling into the ocean! Peter swooped in just in time and rescued her, and then began a fierce duel with Captain Hook. Once again, the evil Hook fell into the water and was chased away by the crocodile—this time forever.

Tinker Bell sprinkled her fairy dust on the ship, and suddenly it was flying through the skies of Neverland, on its way to London. Back in the nursery, Peter Pan and Tinker Bell said good-bye to the children and sailed off into the night. Wendy watched as the beautiful ship sailed past the moon on its journey home to Neverland, the most wonderful land of her dreams.

The Good Little Mouse

Once upon a time, an evil king invaded another kingdom and captured the queen and her infant daughter. He shut them both into the highest room of the tallest tower in the castle. The room was small and empty, with only one table and a very hard bed on the floor. The wicked king sent for a fairy, who was so moved by the prisoners' misery that she whispered to the queen, "Courage, Madam! I think I see a way to help you."

"Silence!" the king cried. He turned to the fairy. "Tell me, is this baby girl destined to grow up to be a worthy bride for my son?"

The fairy answered that the princess would be kind and beautiful. Satisfied, the king declared that the queen would raise the baby in the tower until the girl was old enough to marry his son. Then he took the fairy with him and left the poor queen in tears.

As the days went on, the queen and her baby grew thinner and thinner, for every day they were given only three peas and a crust of black bread to eat. One evening, as the queen sat at her spinning wheel—for she was made to work day and night—she saw a pretty little mouse creep out of a hole. She said to the mouse, "Alas, little creature! Why did you come here? I have only three peas to eat each day, so unless you wish to starve, I'm afraid you must go elsewhere for your food."

But the mouse danced and twirled so prettily that the queen clapped and laughed and gave the mouse her last pea, which she was keeping for her supper.

Suddenly, a delicious meal appeared on the table. The queen was amazed! Quickly she fed her baby and herself and gave the mouse its own share.

The next day, and every day after that, the queen gave the mouse all of the peas, and instantly the empty dish was filled with all sorts of wonderful things to eat. But the queen still worried about the fate of her daughter. The queen despaired and said, "If only I could think of some way of saving her from marrying the horrible prince!"

As she spoke, she noticed the little mouse playing in a corner with some long straws. The queen began to braid the straws, thinking, *If I had enough straws, I could make a basket to lower my baby down from the window. A kind passerby might take care of her and raise her in freedom.*

As she sat braiding, the little mouse dragged in more and more straw, until the queen had plenty to weave her basket. At last, the basket was finished. The queen went to the window to see how long a cord she must make and noticed an old woman far below, looking up at her. The old woman called to the queen, "I know your trouble, Madam. If you like, I will help you."

The queen was overjoyed and told the old woman that she would be rewarded for her kindness.

"I don't care about any reward," the old woman replied. "'But there is one thing I should like. I am very particular about what I eat, and I fancy above all else a plump, tender little mouse. If there happens to be any mouse in your garret, just throw it down to me. That's all I ask."

The queen began to cry. "There is only one mouse in this garret," said the queen, "but I cannot bear to think of its being killed."

"What!" cried the old woman, in a rage. "You care more for a miserable mouse than for your very own baby? Good-bye, Madam! I leave you and your poor daughter to enjoy its company!"

That night, the queen sadly placed the baby in the basket and prepared to lower it into the street. Just then, in sprang the little mouse.

"Oh, little mouse!" said the queen. "It cost me dear to save your life."

Suddenly, the mouse answered, "Believe me, Madam, you will never regret your kindness."

The queen was astonished when the mouse began to speak, and still more so when the mouse suddenly grew into a tall, fair lady. The queen recognized the fairy who had come up to her tower room with the wicked king.

The fairy smiled at her astonished look and said, "I wanted to see if you were faithful and capable of real friendship before I helped you. You see, we fairies are rich in everything but friends, and those are hard to find. I was the little mouse whom you fed when there was nothing to be gained by it. I was the old woman whom you talked to from the window. You are indeed capable of true friendship." Turning to the princess, she said, "Dear little one, I promise you and your mother will be safe under my care. Let us live happily together in my castle, far from here."

The fairy then cast a spell, and all three vanished from the prison room, never to see the wicked king again.

Princess Cat

In ancient China, there lived an emperor with three sons. The emperor was old but did not want to give up his throne, although his sons were old enough to rule. He decided to keep them too busy to think of succeeding him.

The king called his three sons together and told them that he would give up his crown to the son who found him the smallest dog. He gave each of his sons plenty of gold and told them to return in one year.

The eldest prince was disappointed, since the crown would traditionally be passed down to him without competition from his brothers, but he was too polite to argue with his father. The next day, the three princes set out in different directions.

The youngest son was handsome, smart, and very brave. One evening, as he was riding through a forest, a storm suddenly broke. The prince saw a bright light ahead and followed it until he came upon a magnificent palace with walls of crystal and an enormous door encrusted with jewels. When he knocked, the door swung open, and the prince was pulled inside by dozens of invisible hands.

Though uneasy, the prince looked about

and found rich clothes set out for him. Then the hands led him to a dinner table set for two. A beautiful snow white cat entered and introduced herself as Princess Cat. She offered the prince a lavish feast and plenty to drink.

The prince was impressed by Princess Cat's generosity and her marvelous castle. He spent the night, and the next day the prince and Princess Cat played games, hunted in the woods, and picnicked by a waterfall. The prince had so much fun that he stayed the next night, and the next, and the next—until the entire year was almost up.

Luckily, Princess Cat remembered the emperor's contest. She gave the prince a tiny acorn and told him to take it to his father. The prince sadly rode away from Princess Cat's land, already missing her wonderful company.

At the emperor's palace, the two older brothers showed their small dogs. Then it was the young prince's turn. The prince opened the acorn and out jumped a perfect, tiny dog that was no bigger than a snowflake. The dog barked and danced in the palm of the emperor's hand.

The emperor was amazed at his son's gift, but still did not want to give up his throne. He offered his sons the last challenge. After one year, whoever brought back the most beautiful princess in all the land would be emperor.

The prince immediately returned to

Princess Cat. She welcomed him back with a feast and a dance. The pair spent many months fishing, reading aloud, and playing in the woods. As quickly as before, the prince's year was almost up, and he had not yet found a beautiful princess. Resting in front of a fireplace, he asked Princess Cat for advice.

"This is what you must do," Princess Cat said. "Cut my tail off and throw it into the fire."

The prince refused to do as Princess Cat requested. He loved her and did not want to harm her. Princess Cat promised the prince that she would not be hurt and that it would please her. Finally, the prince agreed and shut his eyes as he cut off Princess Cat's tail and threw it into the fire.

Lo and behold! Out of the fireplace stepped a beautiful princess with silken hair and sparkling robes. At that instant, an elegant winged lady flew into the room and embraced the princess. Seeing the prince's confusion, the princess explained that she had been turned into a cat after she refused to wed an ugly magician. The winged lady was Princess Cat's friend, a kind fairy who had ensured that the spell would one day be broken by a prince who loved her dearly.

The prince did love Princess Cat with all his heart, and the pair made plans to marry. The fairy brought the prince and Princess Cat in her flying palanquin back to his father's palace. The emperor was amazed at

Princess Cat's incredible beauty and declared his youngest son the winner of the challenge.

But then Princess Cat interrupted the emperor. "I am the ruler of six kingdoms," she said, "and I would love nothing more than to share those kingdoms with you and your sons." Two kingdoms were given to each prince, and the emperor was overjoyed that he could continue to rule his own. The three brothers wed their princesses, and everyone in the land celebrated their happy marriages for many years to come.

Pinocchio

Once upon a time, there was a piece of wood. The old woodcarver, Geppetto, decided to make it into a puppet named Pinocchio. As he carved the eyes, they seemed to look back at him. When he made the mouth, it opened and laughed at him. And when Geppetto carved two legs, the wooden puppet jumped up and ran away!

On his journey, Pinocchio came to a house that was empty but for a Talking Cricket. The cricket warned the puppet, "Woe to those boys who rebel against their parents and run away from home. They will never come to any good in the world." Because of his hunger more than his conscience, Pinocchio returned to Geppetto and promised to behave and go to school. The kindly old man made school clothes for Pinocchio and even sold his only coat to buy the puppet a schoolbook.

The next morning, Pinocchio was on his way to school when he heard the laughter of a crowd and the beating of drums. He turned from the path to school and followed the noise to a puppet theater. Pinocchio wanted to see the show, but admission was ten cents! And although he promised Geppetto that he would be a good boy, Pinocchio traded his schoolbook for ten cents and went inside! The showman of the theater heard Pinocchio's story about Geppetto's sacrifice and said, "Here are five gold pieces. Go at once and take them to him with my compliments." Pinocchio was overjoyed and thanked the showman a thousand times. On his way back home, the puppet made the mistake of mentioning his newfound riches to Fox and Cat, an unscrupulous pair he met along the path. They chased Pinocchio through the woods, intent on robbing him, until he came to a house where a lovely Fairy with blue hair lived. There he rested in safety, and presently the Fairy came to visit with him. Pinocchio told her his story.

"Where are the gold pieces now?" she asked.

"I lost them!" the puppet lied. Suddenly, his nose grew two inches longer!

The Fairy asked, "Where did you lose them?"

"In the woods," he answered. At this second lie, his nose grew even more.

"Then we shall find them," the Fairy said. Pinocchio became afraid and stammered, "I mean that I swallowed them!" And his nose grew so long that the Fairy laughed at the sight. Pinocchio was so ashamed that he began to cry. After a while, the Fairy clapped her hands and one thousand woodpeckers came through the window and landed on his nose. They pecked at it until his nose was reduced to a normal size. Pinocchio was overjoyed! He thanked the

Fairy and once more started on the path back to Geppetto's house. Again, he was interrupted on his journey, but this time a kind pigeon told him that Geppetto had gone to the seashore to sail to distant lands and find Pinocchio.

Hearing this, Pinocchio felt saddened and guilty. He resolved again to behave and set out for the seashore. However, his lazy and idle nature got him into trouble yet again. He met a boy named Candlewick, who told him of a wonderful land just for boys. "There are no schools, no books, and the week consists of six Saturdays and one Sunday. The boys play from morning to night. That is the country for me! Why don't you come, too?"

Pinocchio said no again and again, but when the coach arrived to take Candlewick to the wonderful land, he could not resist jumping on. Once there, he forgot about Geppetto and the Fairy and spent months playing and making mischief. One day, he woke up and looked in the mirror to find that he had grown donkey ears! He had caught donkey fever because he had been so idle, and soon he would become a whole donkey. The coachman who brought the boys to the land waited for each one to become a donkey, and then he sold them off to be used for work. He lured new boys with the promise of idleness and fun and now was rich from his evil scheme.

Within hours, Pinocchio was a full

donkey and could only bray his sadness. He was quickly sold to a man who brought him to his home close to the seashore. Once there, Pinocchio ran away into the ocean and found that the water transformed him back into a puppet! Delighted, he swam away from his angry owner, farther into the sea.

Suddenly, he was swallowed by a giant fish! Pinocchio was not hurt, but it was dark and frightening inside the fish. Far away, he spied a light. He went toward it and was surprised to find Geppetto, sitting at a candlelit table, eating a small fish! He, too, had been swallowed by the giant fish but could not escape because he didn't know how to swim. They reunited with laughter and tears, and soon tiptoed out of the fish's mouth. Geppetto hung on to Pinocchio's back as the wooden puppet swam to shore.

Once back at home, Pinocchio behaved as well as any real boy could. He went to school, took a job to earn money, and obeyed Geppetto without protest. One night, the Fairy appeared to him in a dream and praised his good deeds. "Well done, Pinocchio!" she said. "You will be rewarded for your good heart." When he awoke the next morning, Pinocchio found that he was a real boy! The rickety old house had also been changed to a warm and comfortable home, and even Geppetto seemed younger and livelier. "This is because of your good behavior," declared Geppetto. They danced with joy, and together they lived happily ever after.

Thumbelina

There was once a woman whose greatest desire was to have a child. She went to see a fairy about her wish and received a flower seed, which she planted that night. The next morning, a beautiful red-and-gold flower with tightly closed petals had grown in the pot. The delighted woman kissed the bud, and suddenly the petals opened. Inside sat a very delicate and graceful little girl. She was the size of a thumb, and so she was named Thumbelina.

Her cradle was a walnut shell, her bed was lined with violet leaves, and she had a rose petal for a blanket.

One night, an ugly toad crept through the window and leaped upon the table where Thumbelina lay sleeping. "What a pretty little wife she would make for my son," said the toad, and she took Thumbelina's bed and jumped through the window with it into the garden.

The toad took the cradle to the pond and placed it on a lily pad, and then went to fetch her son. Thumbelina awoke and cried at finding herself in a strange place with nowhere to go. The fish felt pity for the beautiful girl and nibbled on the lily stem so that she could escape from the toad's ugly son. Away down a stream floated the leaf on which Thumbelina sat, until a may bug picked her up and set her down in a meadow to live among the flowers and grasses.

All through the summer, Thumbelina ate blossom nectar and drank the rainwater that collected on leaves. She wove herself a bed from grasses and sang along with the birds that lived in the trees above. But autumn came, and then winter, and poor Thumbelina grew cold and hungry after the grasses died and the bitter wind began to blow. And when the snow came, each snowflake that landed on her was like a shovelful of snow thrown upon someone our size. Miserably, she left her meadow and wandered in search of food, until she came upon a field mouse's den. Thumbelina begged for a bit of food, and the good mouse took pity on the girl and welcomed Thumbelina into her home, where they lived very comfortably.

One day during the winter, the field mouse told Thumbelina that they would soon have a visitor and that she should prepare her prettiest stories to tell. "He is very rich, with a house twenty times larger than mine," said the mouse. "He is blind, but does very well." And so Thumbelina dutifully recited her best stories and sang her prettiest songs to the visitor, who was a mole. She did not like him, however, because he spoke badly of the sun, the flowers, and all the dear creatures she had lived

with in the meadow. Being a mole, he pre-
ferred to live underground and rarely saw
the daylight.

At the end of his visit, the mole guided
Thumbelina and the field mouse through
one of the tunnels that led to his house. He
warned them that a dead bird lay along the
passage. It was a large swallow with its
wings drawn in tight and its eyes closed.
After the mole and mouse had moved on,
Thumbelina ran back to lay a warm blanket
on the bird, so that even in death it would
not be cold. As she straightened the blanket, she heard a weak *thump thump* in the
swallow's chest. It was alive! Thumbelina
was frightened but returned that night to
cover the swallow with another blanket.

Presently, the swallow awoke. "Thank you, pretty maiden," it croaked feebly. "I have been nicely warmed and shall soon regain my strength." All through the winter, Thumbelina secretly fed and nursed the bird back to health. In the springtime, the swallow prepared to leave the tunnel and asked her to join him, but Thumbelina could not leave the kind field mouse. When the swallow said good-bye and soared into the warm sunlight, Thumbelina felt very sad.

Returning to the field mouse's den, Thumbelina was surprised to see her so excited. "We must start working on your wedding clothes, dear!" said the mouse. "The mole has asked to marry you. You're a very lucky girl." Thumbelina had no choice but to sew a wedding dress. She did not want to marry the mole and live in his underground tunnels. She would miss the sun and the sky, as well as the birds and butterflies who cheered her days last summer.

At last, it was her wedding day. Thumbelina asked permission to stand at the door and say farewell to the daylight. As she stood in the sunshine with her arms raised, she heard a familiar *tweet tweet* overhead. It was her dear swallow! And when he asked her now if she would come with him, she agreed. On and on he flew, until at last he landed near a beautiful lake where a dazzling white palace stood. His nest was among the top of the pillars, but he set Thumbelina down upon a flower of her choosing, where she would be safe.

To her surprise, a tiny man already stood on the flower, with a gold crown on his head and gossamer wings on his back. He was the prince of all flowers and ruled over all the tiny men and women who lived on each flower. The handsome fairy prince was delighted with Thumbelina, as she was the prettiest and sweetest girl he had ever met. He quickly put his crown on her head and asked her to be his wife. This bridegroom was different from the toad and the mole! Thumbelina agreed, and they celebrated their wedding that day. The swallow sang his loveliest song, and the other flower fairies came bearing wonderful gifts for their new princess. The best gift was a pair of fairy wings of her own, so that she could flit from flower to flower as well. Happiness had come to Thumbelina at last, and she and the prince rejoiced at their good fortune until the end of their days.

Little Red Riding Hood

Once upon a time, there was a little girl who lived in a cozy cottage near the edge of the woods with her mother. The girl liked to wear a red cloak with a hood. In fact, she wore it so much that soon she was known as Little Red Riding Hood.

One day her mother said, "Little Red, your grandmother is very sick. Bring her this basket of goodies but be very careful. Keep to the path and no matter what don't talk to strangers."

Little Red Riding Hood kissed her mother on the cheek. "Don't worry, Mama. I'll run all the way to Grandma's without stopping."

Little Red stayed on the path and spoke to no one . . . until she saw a bush full of raspberries. Raspberries were her grandma's favorite! She began picking berries, unaware that a wicked wolf was watching her from the woods.

"What a nice snack she will make," the wolf said under his breath. Just as he was about to pounce, the wolf heard the chopping sound of a woodsman working nearby. "Drat!" he muttered. He needed a plan.

"Where are you going, my pretty girl, all alone in the woods?" the wolf asked, with a toothy grin.

Little Red was so excited about the berries that she forgot her mother's warning. "To see my grandmother!"

"Have you far to go?" asked the wolf.

"Yes," said Little Red Riding Hood. "Her house is all the way on the other side of the woods."

"Well, then," the wolf said, with a little bow. "You had better be on your way."

Little Red Riding Hood skipped down the trail. But the sneaky wolf knew a shortcut. He dashed through the woods until he was at Grandma's door.

Knock! Knock!

"Who's there?" cried Grandma from her bed.

"It's me," said the wolf, trying to make

his voice sound soft and sweet. "It's Little Red Riding Hood. I've brought you a basket of goodies."

"Come in," said Grandma.

The door opened, and a horrible shadow appeared on the wall. "Oh, my!" was all the poor old woman could say as the wolf leapt across the room and grabbed her. He tied her up with rope and put her in the closet.

The wicked wolf put on Grandma's night-clothes and climbed into her bed. Moments later, there was a knock on the door.

"Grandma," called Little Red Riding Hood, "may I come in?"

The wolf tried to imitate Grandma's quivering voice. "Come in!"

Little Red opened the door and set the

basket down, and came closer. "Why, Grandma," she said, "what a deep voice you have."

"The better to greet you with," said the wolf.

"And what big eyes you have."

"The better to see you with."

"And what big teeth you have!"

"The better to *eat* you with!"

The wolf grabbed the girl and let out a sinister howl! His howl was so loud that it echoed through the woods. The woodsman, fearing the worst, grabbed his axe and ran toward the terrible noise. He burst through the door and found Little Red in the wolf's clutches. The woodsman swung his axe! The wolf jumped back, the blade just barely missing him, and let Little Red go.

"I'll get you next time," he said before running off into the woods.

Little Red Riding Hood ran to the closet and untied her grandma as the woodsman looked on.

Later, the three sat down to enjoy the goodies Little Red had brought . . . and she never, ever, *ever* spoke to a stranger again!

The Country Mouse and the City Mouse

There was once a happy little mouse that lived in the country. In the summer, the country mouse scampered around the wheat field, eating grain whenever he felt like it. As the weather grew cold, the little mouse moved into the farmhouse. Inside he gathered nuts and barley that were dropped on the kitchen floor. When winter came, he had a good supply of food in three neat piles: one for nuts, one for barley, and one for crumbs.

One snowy winter day, there was a knock at the door. It was his cousin, all the way from the city! When the little city mouse sat down to dinner, he couldn't believe the country mouse had nothing to eat except barley, nuts, and crumbs.

The city mouse shook his head and said, "My poor country cousin. You do not live well at all. Why, you should see how I live! I have fine things to eat every day."

The country mouse immediately felt ashamed of his simple home.

The city mouse went on, "Tomorrow, we'll go to the city. I'll show you my home and you will see how much nicer it is where I live."

In the morning, they went to the city where the houses were big and there were people everywhere.

The very first place that the city mouse took his cousin was the kitchen cupboard. Inside there was a sack of brown sugar. They began to eat at once. The country mouse had never tasted anything so delicious in his life!

"Wow, cousin," the country mouse said. "You are so lucky!"

Just then, the door swung open with a bang. The city mouse ran for the hole in the corner of the cupboard but the country mouse froze with fear. A cook reached into the cupboard and to her surprise came nose to nose with the country mouse.

She let out a scream and dropped the flour on the floor.

"Don't just stand there, cousin!" shouted the city mouse. "Come on!"

The country mouse scurried through the little hole. When they were safe, the country mouse said, "Whew! That was close."

The city mouse dusted the flour off his whiskers. "Don't worry. She'll be gone soon and then we can go back."

After the cook had gone away, they crept back to the kitchen. This time, the city mouse had something new to share. They went through the hole in the cupboard, where a big jar of dried cherries was left open. These were even better than the brown sugar! Everything was wonderful until they heard *scratch, scratch, scratch* on the cupboard door.

"What is that?" asked the country mouse.

Suddenly there was a loud meow!

The city mouse ran as fast as he could to the hole, and this time the country mouse followed.

As soon as they were out of danger, the city mouse said with a glint in his eye, "That old cat will never catch me! Let's go down to the pantry. There is even more food down there!"

Down in the pantry, there were rounds of cheese, bunches of sausages, and barrels full of pickles. It smelled so good that the little country mouse went wild. He scurried around the room, nibbling a little cheese here and a bit of a pickle there, until he saw a morsel of cheese on a strange little stand in a corner. He was just about to take a big, healthy bite when the city mouse saw him.

"Stop!" cried the city mouse. "That's a trap!"

The little country mouse stopped in his tracks. "What's a trap?"

"That *thing*," said the little city mouse, "is a trap. The minute you touch the cheese, something comes down on your head hard, and—" The city mouse made a loud *clap* with his little hands.

The little country mouse looked at the trap. Then he looked at his cousin. "I think I will go home," he said. "I'd rather have barley and grain and eat it in peace, than have brown sugar and cheese and eat in fear."

The two mice shook hands. The country mouse happily went back to his home. And there he stayed for the rest of his life.

Chicken Little

Once upon a time, Chicken Little was scratching in her garden when an acorn fell out of a tree and hit her on the head.

"Oh, dear me!" she cried. "The sky is falling. I must go and tell the king!"

So she ran and ran until she met Henny Penny.

"Good morning, Chicken Little," said Henny Penny. "Where are you going?"

"Oh, Henny Penny, the sky is falling, and

103

I am going to tell the king!"

"How do you know the sky is falling?" asked Henny Penny.

"A piece of it fell on my head!" said Chicken Little.

"Then I will go with you," said Henny Penny.

So they ran and ran until they met Turkey Lurkey.

"Good morning, Henny Penny and Chicken Little," said Turkey Lurkey. "Where are the two of you going?"

"Oh, Turkey Lurkey, the sky is falling, and we are going to tell the king!" they said.

"How do you know the sky is falling?" asked Turkey Lurkey.

"Chicken Little told me," said Henny Penny.

"A piece of it fell on my head!" said Chicken Little.

"Then I will go with you," said Turkey Lurkey.

So they ran and ran until they met Ducky Lucky.

"Where are the three of you going?" he asked.

"The sky is falling, and we are going to tell the king," answered Turkey Lurkey.

"How do you know the sky is falling?" asked Ducky Lucky.

"Henny Penny told me," said Turkey Lurkey.

"Chicken Little told me," said Henny Penny.

"A piece of it fell on my head!" said Chicken Little.

"Then I will go with you," said Ducky Lucky.

So they ran and ran until they met Goosey Loosey, on her way to the bakery.

"Where are the four of you going?" she asked.

"The sky is falling, and we are going to tell the king," answered Ducky Lucky.

"How do you know it is falling?" asked Goosey Loosey.

"Turkey Lurkey told me," answered Ducky Lucky.

"Henny Penny told me," said Turkey Lurkey.

"Chicken Little told me," said Henny Penny.

"A piece of it fell on my head!" said Chicken Little.

"Then I will go with you," said Goosey Loosey.

So they ran and ran until they met Foxy Loxy.

"My, my. Look at all these plump birds," he said, licking his lips. "Where is everyone going?"

"The sky is falling, and we are going to tell the king," they all replied together.

"But you are not going the right way," said Foxy Loxy, squinting his wicked eyes. "Shall I show you the way to go?"

"Oh, certainly," they all answered at once and followed Foxy Loxy, until they came to the door of his cave among the rocks.

"This is a short way to the king's palace," said Foxy Loxy.

Just as the little feathered folks were

about to follow the fox into his cave, a little gray squirrel jumped out from behind the bushes and whispered to them, "If you go in, that fox will eat all of you!"

The little squirrel threw a big stone and hit the old fox right on the head.

"The sky surely *is* falling," groaned Foxy Loxy, as he fell to the ground. Happy to escape from the wicked fox, the feathered friends thanked the squirrel and continued their journey to see the king.

By and by, they came to the palace where the wise king lived. Upon entering they all shouted at once, "King, we have come to warn you that the sky is falling!"

"How do you know the sky is falling?" asked the king.

"A piece of it fell on my head!" said Chicken Little.

"Come nearer, Chicken Little," said the king and, leaning from his velvet throne, picked the acorn from the feathers of Chicken Little's head. "You see, it was only an acorn and not part of the sky at all," said the king.

Weary but wiser, the little feathered friends left the palace and started on their long journey home.

The Ugly Duckling

One sunny day on a little farm, there was a small pond where a duck was sitting on her nest. Four of the eggs were small, one was much larger than the rest, and all seemed ready to hatch.

The four little eggs cracked open and out popped four little ducklings, yellow as daffodils and pretty as could be. The mother duck was pleased, watching the ducklings peeping about the garden. "Just one more to go," she said, turning her attention to the largest egg of all. But it did not open. So the mama duck waited.

At last the big egg cracked. "Honk, honk!" said the young one. The mother duck gasped, for the largest one was not yellow as a daffodil but an ashy gray. *He must be a turkey*, she thought. *I have an idea. We'll go swimming in the pond. Then I will know for sure.* For every mother duck knows, turkeys cannot swim.

The mother duck went to the water with the five young ones following behind her. She jumped in with a splash. "Quack, quack," she cried. One after another the little ones jumped in. The big one swam the fastest of all.

"Look how well he uses his legs!" said

the mother. "That is not a turkey. He is my own child, and he is not so odd after all . . . if you look at him properly."

After their morning swim, the mother duck took her ducklings to the farmyard to introduce them to the other ducks. Everywhere they went, there was whispering.

"Look how ugly that one is!" the other ducks said.

"Leave him alone," the mother duck scolded. "He is a good creature, and he swims more beautifully than the rest."

But the other ducks on the farm continued to tease him, laugh at him, and call him terrible names. One day, the ugly duckling was just too sad to stay on the farm any longer. He squeezed under the gate and, because he hadn't learned to fly yet, he began to walk away.

Toward evening the ugly duckling reached a poor little cottage that seemed ready to collapse, and only remained standing because it could not decide on which side to fall first. The back door was not quite closed, so he slipped inside and went to sleep.

In the morning, the strange visitor was discovered by a tomcat and a hen. The tomcat purred at the duckling and the hen started to cluck.

"Can you lay eggs?" the hen asked.

"No."

"Can you raise your back or purr?" asked the tomcat.

"No."

"Well," the hen said, "what can you do?"

The duckling thought for a while. "I like to swim," he said.

"What an absurd idea," said the hen. "You have nothing else to do, therefore you have foolish fancies. If you could purr or lay eggs, those thoughts would disappear."

"But it is so delightful to swim," said the duckling.

"Delightful, indeed!" said the hen. "Ask the cat—he is the cleverest animal I know—ask him how he would like to swim about on the water! Ask our mistress, the old woman—there is no one in the world more clever than she is. Do you think she would like to swim?"

"You don't understand me," said the duckling.

"Who can understand you, I wonder? Do you consider yourself cleverer than the cat or the old woman? Believe me, I speak only for your own good. I advise you to lay eggs and learn to purr as quickly as possible."

"I think it's time for me to go," said the duckling.

So the duckling left the cottage and soon found a pond where he could swim and dive. But as winter approached, the air grew colder and colder. The duckling had to swim quickly on the water to keep from freezing, but every night the space on which he swam became smaller and smaller.

In the morning, a peasant found the

duckling frozen to the ice. He broke the ice and carried the duckling home. The peasant and his wife revived the poor little creature. When the peasant's children wanted to play with him, the duckling was frightened. He started up in terror and flew all around the kitchen, knocking over jars of food. The woman shooed the duckling through the open door, and he endured a hard winter all alone.

When spring came, the ugly duckling saw that everything around him had become beautiful. He raised his wings, and, to his delight, he was flying! He rose high into the air and flew until he reached a large garden with a lovely lake. Just in front of him he saw three beautiful swans swimming lightly over the smooth water. The duckling felt more unhappy than ever.

"I want to make friends with them, but I know they will not have me because I am too ugly." Though he was afraid they would reject him, the duckling could not help but swim toward the beautiful strangers. He tried to hide his face by keeping his head bowed, but there, in the reflection of the water, he saw the most curious thing: Another swan was staring back at him. Why, it was him! He was a swan, too. The other swans rushed to meet him with outstretched wings. They stroked his neck with their bills, for this is the way swans say, "Hello."

Soon a boy and a girl came into the garden with corn and pieces of bread, which they threw into the water.

"Look!" shouted the boy. "There is a new one!"

The girl said, "And he is the most beautiful of all!"

The newest swan rustled his feathers and cried out to the boy and girl with joy. And that is the story of the ugly duckling who became a swan.